Soul Moon Soup

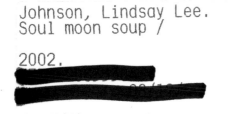

Lindsay Lee Johnson

FRONT STREET

Library of Congress Cataloging-in-Publication Data

Johnson, Lindsay Lee.
Soul moon soup / by Lindsay Lee Johnson.—1st ed.
p. cm.
Summary: After her father leaves and Phoebe and her mother
struggle to survive in the city, Phoebe finally goes to the country
to live with her grandmother, where she learns family secrets
and hopes her mother will return for her.
ISBN 1-886910-87-1 (alk. paper)
[1. Mothers and daughters—Fiction. 2. Grandmothers—Fiction.
3. Single-parent families—Fiction. 4. Homelessness—Fiction.] I. Title.

PZ7.J632526 So 2002
[Fic]-dc21   2002069265

For my Mama and sister Bam
and the memory of our Gram,
all part of the long, strong line of story-spinning,
soup-simmering women in my life.

Soul Moon Soup

Who I Am

Yoo-hoo!
The first thing Mama said
when I was born,
Hoo, baby! Hoo!
You look like an owl!
Whatever will we name you,
my child with wide-open eyes
like two hungry mouths?

Who? Me?

Phoebe, Daddy called me right away.
His bright, shining Phoebe,
born in the middle of a night with a bright, full moon,
like some Greek goddess from a story he knew.
Another one of Daddy's fancies,
Mama says with a sigh
every time she tells the story of my birth.
But I don't mind
being one of Daddy's fancies.
Me, who?
Me, Fancy Phoebe, that's who.

Mama's Fancies

Mama picked my second name,
Rose.
For color, she says, and sweetness.

Mama has a fancy side, too,
but not like Daddy.
Daddy used to let his fancies fly
like flags in the wind.
Mama keeps hers locked up
down deep inside.

I remember a time
Mama let her fancies out
just for me, Phoebe Rose, on my birthday.
Four years old I was
and longing for a cake,
a fine white cake,
two layers or three or four with red-berry filling
and spread all over with thick white frosting,
pink roses on the top,
and four never-burned-before candles
lit just for me,
all in a big white bakery box.

Mama watched me looking at cakes like that
in the wide, wide windows of the bakery store.

She watched me watching other mamas
heading home with cakes like that
all boxed up for their babies.

Don't expect nothing like that
for yourself, she said.

I didn't.

The morning I woke up four years old
there it was,
a big white bakery box
waiting just for me.
Inside I found a cake all right,
a fancy white cake, three layers at least,
pink roses on the top.
It's no eating-cake, Mama said, so don't you try.

Turned out that cake was made of stiff white paper
with tissue-paper flowers, tiny beads and buttons,
and ribbon ringed around,
looped like strings of sugar frosting.
Four pink pipe-cleaner candles poked up on top.
I didn't mind one bit I couldn't eat it.
Eating-cakes just get all eaten up and gone.
Keeping-cakes last.

To think Mama knew how much
I wanted that cake
that she found a way
to take my dream and make it real
with her hands in her own fancy way.

Later Mama showed me how to fold it all flat
so I could keep it packed away.
Somehow, even then I knew it would be a long time
till I saw Mama's fancy side again.

Longing for Home

Keep your eyes open, Phoebe Rose,
Mama says,
and your mouth
shut.

She doesn't have to tell me anymore,
been telling me now a dozen years almost.
Eyes open, mouth shut.
I'm good at it now.
These great big wide-open eyes
don't miss a thing.
The way we live, these eyes
better not ever miss a thing.

The way we live, these eyes
better keep looking out, watching out
to keep getting by.
But all the taking in and soaking up
fills me up so tight,
sometimes I think I'll burst
if I can't let it out
somehow.

Just give that girl a pencil and some paper
and let her draw, Mama says, clam happy she'll be.

I'm not sure about happy.
Clam quiet I think is more like it, because
there's one thing more I want,
one thing more I need to be happy—truly happy.
A small, safe space around me,
like that happy old clam,
a place, the same place every day, a place
to go out from every day and come back to every night.
A place to line up my pencils and my books and my shoes
where nobody touches them,
these things, my things.
A place to hang my drawings on the wall.
A place good enough to bring a friend, my friend,
if I had one.

Home.

I want a home to go home to.

I want to go home.

Necessary Burdens

I'm not sure where we started out.

I know we used to stay with different folks

here and there.

Now we live in the city,

just Mama and me.

We live in the hard poor middle of the city

with a suitcase

on the stoop-sitting, gutter-spitting streets.

The suitcase, Mama says, makes it look like

we're going somewhere.

Looks to me like we're at

the end of the line.

And suitcase or no suitcase,

I don't think we're fooling anybody.

Not even ourselves anymore.

That suitcase is a burden

with its wobbly wheels and zipper off-track.

But it's a burden we have to bear, Mama says.

You lose that suitcase, I'll slap you all the way
to Full Moon Lake.

That's where Mama came from
and she's never been back.
It must have been bad, if this
is better.

Now that suitcase is all we've got.
We used to have more,
but little by little things fell away.
People too.
Some we left behind on purpose, I think.
Others—I don't know.
They used to be with us,
now they're not.

Don't add to my burden, Mama says,
when I take a book about stars
from the church giveaway box.
We have to travel light, she says.
Only what's necessary.

I try not to be a burden.
I try to be necessary.

Remembering Daddy

There was a time Daddy was necessary.
My daddy with his clever-quick, card-trick hands
and belly-deep laugh.

I remember Daddy teaching me to two-step
right on the tops of his shoes.
We sang *On Top of Old Smo-o-o-ky!*
Something about a blue-oo moon.
Those songs all slow and full of sighs,
those were for Mama.
You Are My Sunshine! That was mine.
And *Yeah, yeah, Blue, you good dog you!*
When I get to heaven gonna call for Blue!

If I ever have a dog this side of heaven
I'll tie him tight
so he can't go missing.
For now I draw him over and over
with big brown eyes and a soft wet nose
and a tail that thumps when I sing.
Guess I should have thought to tie him tight,
that daddy, my daddy,
so he couldn't slip away
and gone.

Life with Daddy

With Daddy we lived in a mini-bus
parked in the alley
right where it ran out of gas.
The tires were gone and the radio too.
But we had yellow curtains at the windows
and a bed in the back.

Aren't we lucky? Daddy said.
How many city folks get to go camping?
Camping every day in the city.

Gonna get cold, Mama said,
in the winter.

Don't worry about winter, Daddy said.
We'll be moving on by then.
Don't worry.

Daddy worked long nights, I remember,
Mama and me alone in the bus.
But the more he worked, the less we had.
Payday was the worst.

ll come straight home,
id. Promise.

I will, I swear, I will!

Daddy always came home,
but the money never made it.
Fooled away on his own kind of fun.

A man needs a little fun with his friends,
Daddy said. Some nights
he brought his friends and his fun
right into the bus.

It was all too much for Mama and me,
so we were off to the shelter
for more quiet, less fun.

When we got back, Daddy said,
Looky here!

Perfume for Mama
and a rainbow of pencils for me!
Fun, Mama said,
testing the perfume, is for kids.
Seems like I have two of them now,
one that'll never grow up.

Then Mama looked so faraway tired
like she'd never have the strength

to get where she was going.

I tried to grow fast.

On the Job with Mama

It seemed the more I grew, the more trouble I was.

I needed bigger clothes, bigger shoes,

and I was always in the way,

Mama's way.

I used to go off to work

with Mama, cleaning houses

for people who had them.

Okay to bring my baby? Mama'd ask. She's quiet.

So room after room Mama cleaned those houses

filled with beds and tables and chairs, and toys and clothes,

TVs as big as the back of a bus.

And so much food!

Mama said it mostly went to waste.

The prancy poodles and flat-faced cats in those houses

ate so much they threw it up on the rug

or turned up their noses altogether

at handouts I'd like to have handed out to me.

So we helped ourselves now and then.

But the bigger I got, the less welcome I was

in those houses.

My girl's no trouble, Mama said,

she won't touch a thing.

She draws, just sits and draws.

But the people in the houses frowned.

My girl knows how to clean, Mama said when I was bigger,

she'll be extra help, no charge.

But the people in the houses said no,

no children on the job.

So little by little we quit.

I didn't mind.

I could see it wore Mama out,

not the work so much as all those things.

So much too-much that we'd never catch up

with the least of it.

Doodles

Doodles, Mama called my drawings.

Don't burden me with your doodles, she'd say.

I remember Mama crying one time

that she didn't have a dress,

not a thing fit to wear,

not even underwear all in one piece.

People think you're stupid or crazy, Mama said,

and definitely lazy

if you can't turn yourself out

with a shine.

So I made up a closetful of dresses for Mama,

some for fun with sparkles and stripes

and dancing shoes to match,

others with buttons down the back.

Even underwear.

I drew them up with all my best colors,

cut them out careful

for a special surprise,

and gave them to Mama.

What earthly good are these doodle clothes to me?

Phoebe Rose, you think

I'm some paper-doll mama with no-muss hair

and a pasted-on smile?

She tossed them right out, every one.

I knew she couldn't wear them.

I just wanted her to see what I'd give her

if I could.

She never even saw the very best one

with rainbows on the skirt

and glitter on top.

My favorite.

But Daddy looked—really looked—at my pictures
and he smiled.
My drawing made him happy,
not just a picture of the big comfy cuddle-up chair
we'd never have,
but my idea of that chair I made and showed him.
My taking the chair in my mind
and making it on paper
and giving it to him.

I do believe you're coming up
to be a real true artist, Phoebe Rose, he told me.

Don't encourage her, Mama said.

Daddy shrugged. Better listen to your mama.
But the light in his eyes when he looked at that chair
made me wish being a real true artist
was necessary.

Off to School with Secrets

You're too big for doodling, Mama said
when I turned six.
It's time you're off to school.
Not baby-sitting, getting-ready play school.

It's time for big, going-every-day school,
for some real, pay-attention
kind of learning.

Big school, I learned, is another place to keep quiet,
a place to keep secrets.

Don't talk about standing in line
for macaroni cheese suppers at the shelter
or our everlasting suitcase.
Don't go home with other children.
Don't show around those doodles of all we don't have.

She didn't have to tell me.
And I didn't have to show any pictures
to tell what we didn't have.
My own same clothes every day after day
told the story plain as can be.

You're not the only one, Mama said.

But that didn't help.
Being one of a whole lot of down-and-outers
didn't cheer me up one bit.
I saw other kids like me at school now and then.
Shelter kids don't talk at school.
What's to say?

Secrets of the Shelter

I especially hated the way we'd start the day
rounded up for school on the shelter bus.
All around the city it went,
stopping for the kids who slept mat to mat
in the basements of churches
and empty buildings nobody wants.

The best places had blankets,
bathrooms with real flushing toilets,
sinks with mirrors on top.
At St. Steven's everybody got
a three-minute turn in the shower
and a chance to wash one load of clothes.

The worst place was the old animal testing lab.
Once it was a place for squirting
hairspray into rabbits' eyes
to see how many squirts it took
to make them blind.
Wouldn't want the ritzy ladies
getting hurt on their hairspray.

Now those torture rooms are places
for poor folks to sleep, the lucky ones.
Some people with money for the tickets

play to take a chance
on the money-winning lottery.
At the shelters we played for free
to take a chance
on the mat-on-the-cold-tile-floor-winning lottery.

I felt guilty when we won,
seeing the look in the eyes of other mamas
packing up their snot-nosed babies
and setting off seventeen blocks
to the next slap in the face.
I felt worse when we lost.

There's good luck and bad luck, the lottery lady said.
Everybody gets their share
of both.
That's what makes it fair.

I said, If one person's good luck
has to be another person's bad luck,
it spoils things for everybody.
Luck, I decided, is nothing
to depend on.

One thing even the winners never got:
privacy.

Shelter life was always
share and share alike.
Not just with other folks.
Shelter life was R and R,
a little rest and relaxation
with the roaches and the rats.

Then it was early up and out for the special
poor-kids breakfast in the school cafeteria.
All the cereal, bread, applesauce, and milk
came wrapped or boxed in little packages.
I don't remember ever
seeing Mama cook.

One time my locker partner gave me
a bottle of shampoo,
a pink bar of soap, and a washcloth
all tied up together pretty as you please.
It's from my mother, I don't care,
she told me, backing off
when I threw the stuff away.

I slipped out of social studies early
to see if I could find that priceless
treasure in the trash,
but it was gone.

Now, who could I talk to
about a thing like that?
A sister, I guess,
if I had one.

Mama Comes to School

I remember the last time Mama came to school
like she did every couple of whiles.
Another new teacher. Another new school. Again.
Mama held herself so stiff and tight
I thought she might break if I touched her.
I showed her my desk and my report on Spain,
where the sun shines so bright and hot
people nap in the day
and dance in the night.
They eat spicy-hot pork and rice
and sweet three-milk cake for dessert.

Mama didn't drink the punch or even eat a cookie.
I can't stay long, she said to the teacher.
We're in the middle of moving, been staying with kin.
We'll have our own place soon.
My mouth flew open, and stuck
till Mama closed it with a look.
That story of Mama's made me feel

like April Fools' Day could be
any old day of the year.

I should know better by now,
but I fall for Mama's stories
every time.
Just for a second I think,
Maybe this time it's true.
Maybe Mama's been saving
this good big news for me. A surprise!
And this is her way of springing it.

Hearing what I wish for so bad
jump-starts that little-bitty engine of hope
inside, revving it up
for a heartbeat, then
with Mama's sideways glance
it stalls.

No, Mama said,
I don't have the address yet, the phone's not in.
It won't be long.

It's not really a lie,
Mama told me later.
Just telling folks what they want to hear.
It's called getting by.

Teacher looked at Mama like she was an injured bird,
one that might peck
if she poked too much.
Anything I can do? Teacher asked.

Mama locked up her face.
Just teach my girl the good, necessary things
she needs to know to make her way
in this world so hard.
She can't live on daydreams
like she learned from her daddy.

Looking at Mama,
Teacher didn't dare
ask about Daddy.

Necessary and Gone

Daddy had already disappeared by then,
ripped away like a page from a book.
It hadn't taken long
for the words of his songs to fade
like a sunset deep inside me.
The blue moon and the dog
started to fade from my mind
along with Daddy's face,

Daddy's voice,
Daddy's long, quick fingers.
All he left was the ring on Mama's hand.

At least she got that.
All I got is nothing.
A big old hole full of nothing
where my daddy used to be.
Was it my fault he left? Was I too much trouble?
Nobody explains anything to me.

Everything was too much trouble
for your daddy, Mama says.
He was just a good-times daddy, so forget him,
Phoebe Rose. That man's gone.

I say to Mama that my daddy might still be with us
if she'd been a little nicer
instead of picking away at everything he said,
everything he did or didn't do.

That's the way you feel, Phoebe Rose,
maybe you should have gone off with him, Mama says.

Mama's words land like a punch in my stomach.
Is that what Mama wishes?
Is that what Mama wants?

Moving On with Mama

First we lost Daddy;

the mini-bus went next,

hauled away in the middle of the night.

The yellow curtains and the bed,

my rainbow of pencils,

Mama's perfume,

all hauled away in the night by some not-nice men—

we don't know who.

They made us leave in the dark of the night,

just Mama and me,

with our suitcase packed hurry-up and out.

We'd always gotten by

before...

But there was no room at Aunt Char's

since her twins were born.

Mrs. Brownmiller and her lumpy daybed

had gone to the old folks' home.

And the waiting list for

broken-down,

bug-crawling,

no-hope apartments

was too long to wait for.

Some places, Mama said, are worse

than no place at all.

So now we make a meal of free apples

brown-bruised from the fruit man,

yesterday's bread left in the alley,

soup,

when the shelter has enough to go around.

We make our bed on a bench,

in a box, or a doorway,

wherever we are when sleep comes.

Lucky days bring coins left in telephones,

lost gloves found at the bus stop,

a nap snatched at the laundromat

to the hum of the heat-thumping dryers.

But lucky days are running out

in the mean dirty city,

where the hungry eyes of strangers watch,

where the quick hands of strangers wait

to take their chance,

my chance,

my shoes,

my soul.

Get a job, people say to Mama. Earn your way.

They say it mean.

And Mama tries to hide it, but it hurts,

I can see it in her eyes.

But the people with the jobs
ask where she lives.
The people with apartments
ask where she works.
It costs more to live than any job will ever pay
to my mama.
So we keep moving on to avoid all the questions.
The social service people have
too many rules, too much paperwork,
they make you pay with promises
and answers.
If we had the answers,
we wouldn't need the help.
So we keep on moving on.

Going Blank

While Mama knocks on slamming-shut doors
I wait curb-crouched and low
in the shadow of tower-tall buildings
that shoulder out the sky.
To pass the lonely time
and keep the jittery, jumpy, boogey thoughts away
I draw no-color pictures on paper-bag scraps
with half-used pencils
till they rub down to stubs.
Then I make up songs for myself.

But the air is so thick and sour and loud
I can't hear myself think or sing
or wish on a star—
not even in my dreams anymore.

I used to have dreams, big dreams—
me, Phoebe Rose, tap-dancing on Broadway,
singing on MTV,
putting on a one-woman show in a real art gallery,
buying a genuine house for my mama
and a sweet, whisker-faced pooch
for me.
All those ideas burst in my head
like fireworks
shooting up so high,
the colors exploding so fast,
I thought they'd never end—
but they're gone.
The daydreams and nightdreams disappeared
like a TV screen gone blank.

I don't know how to fix it myself,
I don't want to be a bother,
so I don't say a word. I wait
for some spark, some signal, to return.

Fading Fast

I keep on moving.
What else can I do?
But deep inside I'm slowing down,
down deep inside I'm shutting down,
closing down, turning into
nothing.

Nothing
is good, I think.
How simple life would be
if I could fade away to
nothing.

Fading is easy at first.
All you do is sit
and little by little
it happens.
Don't make noise,
don't ask for food,
don't even think. Just fall
into that deep, dark lake
in your soul and sink.

Nobody notices.

Little by little I'm disappearing
from the inside out.
It makes life easier for everybody
when I don't ask questions,
don't make a ruckus,
don't need don't want don't expect
one single thing.

Why's your girl gone so quiet?
asks a lady handing out toothpaste at the shelter.

Mama looks surprised,
like she hasn't noticed.
Hasn't noticed I am done with talk,
done with dreams,
done with my everlasting doodles.
Hasn't noticed if I am here
or gone.
Just getting to that age,
Mama says with a lift of her eyebrows
that shrugs me off her mind.

Inside I'm still
kicking and screaming a little
but fading fast.
So Mama goes on thinking what she's thinking,

and the lady at the shelter
moves on, and life keeps getting easier
for everybody.

Teacher Trouble

I never make trouble
at school. Trouble makes its own self.
Today the teacher,
not the regular one, a sub, says,
Draw a picture
of what you want to be,
what you want to do
with your life in the future.

The kids all around me get busy, so busy,
all bent over papers, colored pencils held tight
till our time is up.
Then that teacher gets mad, so mad,
at my no-picture picture,
at me.

Don't you listen?
Haven't you learned a thing
about art all this year?
Or are you just lazy?

Don't tell me you can't think of a thing to draw,
there's nothing you want to be.
You're a big disappointment,
young lady.
Teacher said you were an artist.
Do you think you'll get by
doing nothing for a sub?
Do you think it doesn't count for your grade?

She gets so red in the face,
taps her foot, taps her pencil, and waits
for nothing.

Want me to post your paper
on the wall with the others?
That make you proud?
Okay, she says, and up it goes
on the wall with the astronauts
and doctors
and the rock stars
and the chefs.
My big blank paper, I think,
is perfect.
That's me, Phoebe Rose,
in the bright shining future:
invisible.

The Last Burden Falls Away

Wait right here, Mama says,
in front of the bus station,
hold on to the suitcase,
don't move till I get back.
I want to do what Mama tells me,
but she's gone a long while
and I have to use the toilet real bad.

I know my way around; we pass a lot of time here.
We're never truly waiting
like the real bus-riding folks. But sitting with a suitcase
while the people and the buses
come and go looks fine, Mama says.
Only the others passing time, like us,
not waiting for a bus,
they're the only ones who know you don't have a ticket.
Those are the ones to watch, Mama says,
but not straight on,
only from the corner of your eye.

In the bathroom
the stalls are too tight with that ever-blessed suitcase,
and the one wide door of the wheelchair stall is locked.
But I can't wait.
I don't want to worry Mama, disappearing

from the spot where she said to stay.
So I scuttle to the shower stall,
sideways like a crab, dragging on that suitcase,
and I squat right over the drain.

I want to wash the smell away, so
I turn the shower on, just a tiny turn,
but it blasts full force, icy cold on my head,
then hot, too hot, on the suitcase.
God help me save the suitcase! I pray.

I open the door quick and shove
that wobbly, wretched bag out fast.
It squeals loud as it goes
all skittery and jerky across the cracked wet tile.

I turn my back just a second
to stop that blasting water,
and in that second it is gone.
That all-important, ever-present burden of our lives
is gone.

There's one thing Mama counts on me for,
to be the keeper of the suitcase,
just that one thing she needs me for,
and I let that suitcase slip away.

Without that suitcase to hold me down
I can't walk straight, think I might blow away
down the street
like a cartoon tumbleweed.
But nobody's laughing.
Not me.

Back on the curb I wait for Mama,
wet and cold on the outside,
just plain blank on the inside.

I can't see the next thing, can't imagine
what might come next.
I already know
that Mama placed more value on the suitcase
than she did on Daddy.
Now I'll find out if that suitcase truly was
her last burden,
if it was the baggage
or me.

What Comes Next

Soon enough Mama shows up
with a couple of tiny little giveaway size
ice cream cones from a grocery store.

Lick it up fast, Phoebe Rose, before it melts.

When I don't reach out or even look up
at her face, Mama sees that it's gone.
The suitcase.

The tiny little cones go splat on the street
and I feel Mama's hands,
so strong around my shoulders,
pull me up and shake like she expects
to shake that suitcase right out of me
like salt from a shaker
if she shakes hard enough,
but I'm empty.

Mama's never hit me much before,
but I don't really mind the slapping.
The worst is the wailing
Mama makes
while she drags me up and down the rows
of chairs in the bus station,
through alleys, under bridges,
searching for what's lost
and can't be found.
I know Mama put so much store in that
all-important suitcase

and I hate that it's gone
with our last clean socks
—and my cake.
I couldn't even keep hold of my keeping-cake!

It's all my fault.
Still, I don't think Mama should be
carrying on like she is,
on and on so fierce and pulling at her hair.
I want her to stop,
but I don't dare say a word.

The only words I hear from Mama
between the wails
make no sense to me.

My baby's hair!
My baby's hair!
A lock of baby's hair
was zipped inside
a secret pocket in the suitcase!
Now I've lost the last only thing
I had to remember
my baby!

Now she's crumpled right down to the street.
My mama, poor mama,

looks to be running out of steam.
So I sit down beside her
and stroke her head
like she does for me
when I'm down with a fever
or my stomach turns bad.
Don't worry, I say to my mama.

But losing that suitcase was the one last thing,
the one last straw too much for my mama.

Don't worry, I tell her again and again.
We'll get another suitcase somehow.
We'll fill it up again
with the things we need.
I'll get a rope and tie it tight to my wrist
next time, I promise.
It'll never get away from me again.
Okay?

Mama starts up the wailing
but softer now and sobbing
about that hair, her baby's hair.
I never knew she kept a snatch of hair
from my baby head. Even though I never saw it
I like knowing that she had it.

I like to imagine the little dark curl of it
with a pink ribbon bowed around it.
In my mind I can see it now
even though it's gone.

It's okay, I tell my mama.
I know it's not the same, but
I still have a whole head of hair
for you.
I'll cut off a good snip and tie it up pretty
for you.

Then Mama lifts her head
and looks at me
like she doesn't know
who I am.

The End of the Day

At the end of the day
the crowded streets empty out.
So many people, heading for home.
We should be heading for the shelter
to claim our place for the night.
But Mama keeps on sitting, just sitting and looking
at nothing.

What's wrong with us, Mama?
Are we lost?

We're so lost! Mama says,
her head in her hands.
We're down to nothing but pride.

I search Mama's eyes for tears,
but they're dry. Pride?

Stubborn pride, your Gram said when I left home.
I guess I got it from her
and it's all I got.
Pride makes a hard pillow and a bitter meal.
I can't go back like this, can't raise you on pride.
Phoebe Rose, it's time to let you go.

Please, Mama!
Don't leave me off with strangers!
Mama, please!
I'll get us another suitcase! I will!

It isn't the suitcase, Phoebe Rose,
and your Gram's no stranger, you'll see.
Besides, it's not for keeps, just for the summer,
till I make a new start
and you're back to school again.

Now it already seems like Mama is fading,
or maybe it's me.
All I can do is sit, sit and look
at nothing.

There'll be stars in the sky at Gram's,
Mama says.
Make a wish on a star for me.

Good-bye to the City

No use to protest,
now I'm one of the people on the bus with a ticket.
I always hoped one day I'd ride with a ticket,
but not like this,
not without Mama.

I'll come for you soon, Mama says.

Is that a promise? A real true promise?
Don't forget! Don't forget to remember!

Mama's face is at the window,
her hands at the glass.
Now the wide gold band is gone.
Sold to buy a ticket on the bus.

Mama waves, growing smaller,
then she's gone.
Mama's face, Mama's fingers, Mama's wide gold ring,
swallowed by the hard mean city
and gone.

All night long I sleep dreamless sleep too deep to dream,
all night long on the bus
till the deep night turns to day.
Now the city is gone and the country has come.
I don't know myself
here at all.

No bus station here,
just a stop on the side of the road.
The door wheezes open and Gram is here,
a tiny wire of a woman in a faded-out dress
and cowboy boots, toes turned tips up.
This Gram has hair too black to believe,
streaked here and there with white and bunched
on the back of her head.
Her teeth have all ganged up
at the front of her mouth like each one's
trying to be the first one seen.
I rub sleep from my eyes
to study this Gram.

When she smiles I think I see
my mama.

Child, Gram says with stretched-out arms,
my sleepy-eyed, rib-boned child.
You've been so long in the hard cold city,
you've turned nearly all to stone. Well,
I'll fix that.

Hello to the Country

Gas station store church tavern café.
A few little houses.
That's all I see in what Gram calls town.
The country is too far for walking, Gram says,
so we ride in the back of a neighbor's car.
It's Walter at the wheel and Deena at his side.
Hey there, Phoebe Rose, they say
with open faces just as friendly as can be.
Come meet our gang of kids when you want,
when you're ready, Deena says.
Our middle girl's got the jimmies
just waitin' for you.
Come meet our goats and our rabbits,
Walter says, grinning wide
with his one gold tooth winking at me
in the rearview mirror.

I don't have any words to say
about meeting goats and rabbits
or girls in the country.
I wonder what I'm doing here,
how long I'll have to stay.

All in good time, Gram answers for me,
all in the fullness of time.

After a long twisty ride we come to a dip in the road.
The car slows down and we pull into Gram's yard.
Walter and Deena give me a small sack of peanuts
and a candy bar. My stomach
feels empty and full of knots,
like it's been going round
too long on a merry-go-round,
so I'm glad to get out and wave good-bye.

Welcome to Gram's

This is it, Gram says,
showing me around her place.
Not much, but it's all I need.

Not much? It looks plenty fine to me.
But different, so different from the city,

so much light, so much air,

so quiet—

another world, another planet.

Am I dreaming, am I dead?

Tucked in the trees Gram has a whole little house to herself.

A whole tiny little doll's house

painted yellow, shutters blue, chimney red.

It looks awful rickety, especially the porch,

but that's wide enough to hold a pair of rocker chairs.

Then I see the lake,

the terrible Full Moon Lake

I've always heard about and feared to see.

It's round like a coin, silver smooth on top,

rippled here and there by a breeze.

Just a little puddle of a lake, Gram says,

but the water is sweet and cool.

Dead, I decide, that's what I must be,

never had a dream like this.

But is this heaven or the other place?

They ought to put a sign out front

so you'd know.

Maybe it's true they try to trick you.

I decide to take it slow.

Easing In at Gram's

At Gram's little place on Full Moon Lake
the whole wide world throbs green.
I dig in the soft, fresh, worm-worked earth,
I warm in the gentle sun.
When rain comes down from the great wide sky,
it's not dirty tears like the rain in the city
but a soft shower bath from low-floating clouds
like sponges wrung to puddles.
I learn the joy of mud.
I feast on sweet, maple-syrup-soaked corncakes,
plump fish fried crisp and buttery,
snapping in Gram's spider pan.
Eat up, Gram says, eat your fill.

My eyes slide away
when neighbors come to call.
They bring smiles and songs and pans of apple brown Betty.
This used to be your mama's favorite, Gram says,
join in, help yourself.

But I can't keep myself from holding back.
I don't want to think about Mama, that mama
who sent me off like a dog to the pound,
where I'm safe and warm and fed
and so low-down, hollowed-out sad
I could howl!

Floddie

As long as I have to be stuck in the pound
at Gram's I was hoping for a dog
to share all my sorrows,
not a prancy poodle, a real true tail-thumping dog.
But the closest thing she's got
is a big gray shadow of a cat
named Floddie.

She just showed up one night, Gram says.
Such a scrawny old cat!
One eye gone blank and ears gone raggedy
from too many winters
left out in the cold.
From the looks of that saggy old baggy
jungle pouch of a belly,
she was nearly spent
turning out batches of babies, Gram says.
But still she's got a purr.

About cats I'm not so sure.
The only ones I've known
are the fake-rich-cushion type of cats
or the ragbag scared-of-people type of cats
chasing rats through the trash in the alley.
I decide to let Floddie make

the first move.
After licking and washing and cleaning herself
from whisker to tail,
she slides up sideways slow.
I pass the sniff test,
so Floddie plunks herself down heavy
in my lap like she plans to stay.

That Floddie likes a lap all right, Gram says.
Looks like she's claimed yours, Phoebe Rose,
hope you don't mind. Once she's decided
that's pretty much it.

I don't say yes or no,
but I pretty much like being chosen,
even by a raggedy-eared, one-eyed, worn-out
cat.

The Crimson Ladies

Then there are those chickens,
running all around
like...chickens!
I never saw a live one before
with its feathers still on
and its head. Gram calls them

the Crimson Ladies.

Not a daddy chicken in sight around here.

Too much bother, Gram says,

too loud and proud for my trouble.

I learn it's hard to make friends with a chicken,

they don't cozy up,

so I keep my distance and get out of their way

when they want to peck

at the ground I'm on.

After a few blows to my sneakered toes

Gram's cowboy boots make sense.

Those Crimson Ladies own the yard, Gram says.

Even Floddie doesn't mess

with those chickens.

I never imagined chickens would be anything

but silly, running round on stick-skinny legs,

bobbing little wild-eyed, pea-sized heads.

But these Crimson Lady birds of Gram's are dressed

so fine. I pick up dropped feathers

they leave here and there like streaks of fire,

like blood.

All the ritzy ladies stepping in and out

of taxis in the city would cry

for a dress like these ladies wear every day
just to scratch in the dirt at Gram's.

They even pay their own way,
the Crimson Ladies.
Each one puts out an egg
every day, each one in her own nesting box
in the rusty old dusty splinter-board
chicken-wire coop.
Gram keeps what eggs she needs
and sells the rest
for cash.
I've seen the big old wad of it
on the very top shelf of the sideboard,
back behind the pie plates, folded in a blue coffee can.
Gram thinks she's hiding it there safe
from sneaking, snatching, no-good thieves.
I guess she doesn't worry
what these wide-open eyes of mine
might see.

Getting Ready for Wishing

Late after sundown
sudden dark is split by owl scream.
Gram pulls me close and together we wait,

in the night lit by fireflies,
past cricket hum and frog song,
watched by the squinty-eyed moon.

Suddenly the stars break through,
salting the bright black night
with wishes.
So many stars!
Which one is for Mama?
So many stars!
There must be one for me!

Make a wish, Gram says.

I answer with a shrug.
What do you wish for when you haven't got a thing,
not inside or out?
Not a daddy or a mama or a place to call home.
No words, no wishes, no hope.

There's no rush, Gram says,
the stars will wait,
they'll be here every night
just waiting till you're ready for some wishing.

I'm glad Gram doesn't push,
just holds my hand and whistles in the dark,

waiting with me
while I wait
for hope to return.

I study Gram close and see
she doesn't have that fake sweet smiley
can't-wait-till-you-leave-so-I-can-let-my-face-down
sort of look.
But you never can tell right away.
All the witches in the stories are nice at first.
And this is where I've landed
for doing the last worst thing.
Slapped all the way to Full Moon Lake.
So I have to be careful,
take my time with Gram.

Just in Case

I have to make plans, just in case,
in case Gram is a witch, not an angel,
in case Mama doesn't come like she said.
I'll give them till my birthday
—that Mama, that Gram—
till my number-twelve birthday
way deep down in August.
If Mama's not back for me by then

she's not coming.

Then it's up to me to go looking

till I find her, that Mama,

find out if she's sick, if she's hurt,

if she needs me, if she wants me,

if she ditched me,

if she's dead,

or I've gone down and don't even know it.

Nobody tells me anything important.

I'll have to run till I know for myself.

Seems crazy,

if this place of Gram's is as fine as it seems,

a little bitty heaven of a place,

why would Mama run from heaven?

Why would I?

Will I?

I will.

Ruby

Then there's Ruby!

Walter and Deena's girl from across the lake

said she couldn't wait

any longer for me to come to her,

so she came to me.

Ruby, just a year ahead of me, with short, tight braids

and a face made for smiling,
one cheek dimpled deep like a button in a belly.

At first I'm shy, like hope itself,
needing to be coaxed and lured like a skittery pup.
Hope and me, we don't jump out all at once
from behind a bush like hide-and-seek
and all in free.
We sit off at a distance
and move in slow.

But Ruby can't stop moving and talking
and pulling at me
inside and out
with crazy stories and riddles and ideas
so big I can't keep on
holding back.

Look at this, Ruby says.
She hands me a clump of moss.
Look close.

So I look at this scrap of damp green carpet,
and pretty soon I see a tiny velvet forest,
a tangle of roots and runners like hands
that grab ahold of nubby rough bark, cracked shingles,

even cold bare rock.
I lift it to my nose and smell
the earth and all the living things that begin and end
in the mud.
I think if I could look close enough I could see
tiny creatures
carrying on their living and their dying
and everything in between,
all on this tender little clump of toad-high moss,
green moss so green,
the color of a promise, of life,
of hope.

Here's what I like about moss, Ruby says.
You can pinch up a piece from here
and plunk it down there
and it goes on growing just as easy and as happy
and as pleased with itself
anywhere.

At last,
Ruby cracks me open
and I let her in to be my friend.
Nearly like the sister I never had,
my friend Ruby.
Ruby doesn't mind about missing mamas

or disappearing daddies.
She doesn't look funny at my clothes
or ask too many questions.
Ruby wants to sing and dance and play
with me, Phoebe Rose, her friend.

Daring to Draw

Ruby comes to see me at Gram's
with thick pads of drawing paper,
pencils, crayons, and fat sticks of chalk.
Phoebe Rose, you like to draw?

I shrug. How about you?

Better than anything!
Hope to learn enough to be a teacher
someday.

Ruby, you think art is that important,
in a necessary way?
You sure it's not some fluffy decoration
on the true necessary things in life,
like a ruffle on a dress?

Not for me, Phoebe Rose.
Some people figure things out

with numbers. For me,
it never adds up to make sense.
I have to think about questions
with pictures
and draw out the answers that way.
Art is the best way
for me to know things.
I guess that makes it necessary
for me.

Ruby lets me watch, moving closer, while she draws
shadowy cattails, pussy willows, milkweed pods
so real you can feel them
with your eyes.
Ruby's good at faces too. The way she draws
the two of us, we look alike,
the same, but each in our own way.
I like to think we do.

Watching Ruby draw I start to feel pictures
in my head that want to come out.
But I'm just too tired,
and the feelings I feel
hurt so much—that's why I stopped—
and now there's so awful much inside
that's all broken up and hurt
I'm scared to let it out.

To Ruby I say,
My daddy used to sing the pictures in his head.
If I don't sing what I feel, Daddy said,
I'll choke.
Now I know that feeling and I think
it might be easier
to choke.

Ruby says,
What songs do you know, Phoebe Rose?

I try to remember the blue moon song,
but it seems too sad
for Ruby.

We can make a new blue moon song,
Ruby tells me,
a jumpy new blue moon song
with a brand-new name.

I pick out a crayon the color of magic,
the color of dreams so deep you know they're real.
Indigo.
We call it our Indigo Moon song.

Under the Indigo Moon,
under the Indigo Moon,

we eat soup with a fork and cake with a spoon,
under the Indigo Moon.

Under the Indigo Moon,
under the Indigo Moon,
we make mudpies in December and snowballs in June,
under the Indigo Moon.

Under the Indigo Moon,
under the Indigo moon,
we wear stars in our hair and sing out of tune,
under the Indigo Moon.

Under the Indigo Moon,
under the Indigo Moon,
we laugh all night and sleep till noon,
under the Indigo Moon.

Drawing Again

At last I can draw!
I draw my pictures,
all the pictures stuck so long in the city,
so stuck in my head.
They're not pretty.
Ugly, hard, nasty picture after picture pours out

till my fingers ache.
I see myself on paper,
a mean, cruel monster sending Mama away in tears,
the same as Mama did to me.

At last I take a deep breath,
such a deep, ragged breath, I must have nearly stopped
taking air.
I nearly forgot how
to breathe.
Now my head is clear and free,
in a scary sort of way, wide open and ready,
nothing left to lose,
nothing left to fear.

Watching me and Ruby, Gram says,
You're clever like your mama as a girl,
so full she was
of cat's cradle, daisy chains, and jumprope chants.

Gram's words make my heart leap!
Still I don't know what to think, how to feel, what to say
about Mama.

Making Jam with Gram

The days slide by in the country and I settle in.
We get used to each other,
Floddie, the Crimson Ladies, Gram,
and me.

By the middle of July
the raspberries swell so fat on the canes
they drop at the touch of a hand.
Every day we eat our fill
of the bumpy bright red globes
of fuzzy fruit that explode in your mouth
with a squash of your tongue.

Still there's plenty left for jam, Gram says.

I never knew people made it
for themselves.

Gram shows me how
to load those berries in a kettle on the stove
and cook them in sugar water,
mash them, cook them down
to thick red syrup.

Some of the syrup we pour into jars boiled hot,
too hot to touch, then top it off

with hot melted wax that cools to a seal.
A dozen little jars lined up
on Gram's kitchen counter.
Jam! Homemade!
By Phoebe!

The rest of the syrup Gram ties in a bag
of wide-open, waffle-weave cheesecloth.
She hangs it up to drip slow red drops,
clear ruby-red jelly in a bowl,
leaving the seeds behind.

While we wait for the last
of the drippy red drops to drip,
Gram starts to leak stories,
the stories of her life.

A late bloomer, Gram calls herself.
Married late to the grandaddy I never knew—
too late, they thought,
for babies.
Till along came my mama.

Such a happy late surprise, Gram says,
like extra icing on the cake
for us.

But sometimes late's too late.
With this one chance to be a mama
I wanted real bad to get it right.
I was strict, I was hard,
didn't budge with our baby.
Maybe I didn't know
what a mama's supposed to be.

Your mama, Phoebe Rose, was in such a hurry
to be grown up and on her way,
she wouldn't listen, wouldn't wait to finish school,
it all had to be right now.
She left home too young
with a no-good bum,
not your daddy
but a different no-good bum
with no schooling, no job, no ambition
to make a respectable person of himself.
He got your mama hooked on a bad way of living
that looked like fun at first
but was more like
dying real slow.

I don't like this story
and I wonder if it's true
or if it's some strange story-telling ways

they do here in the country,
something I don't know from the city,
so I listen with doubting ears.

Finally that first bum of your mama's
got himself in some deep
kind of trouble and jail.
By then your mama had a little baby girl,
a baby girl she couldn't care for, couldn't keep.
Your mama had to give her up, that first baby girl,
to some folks able to give her a proper home.

This must be crazy witch-talk!
My mama had a baby
before she had me?
With a different daddy
before my daddy?
That means I have a sister!
Had a sister, almost.
I have a million questions I want to ask,
but I don't want to know.
How could that mama, my mama,
our mama,
have a whole different life,
a different daddy for her baby, different baby,
and give that baby away?

With never a say-so about it
to me.
If she did it once
she might do it again
to me.
Maybe she's already done it
to me.

More Sorry Secrets

But Gram keeps on talking
like she has to get it out
before she changes her mind.
So I sit on my questions and listen
to the secrets, the big sorry secrets of my life.

Then along came your daddy, Gram says,
then you, Phoebe Rose.
Your mama was happy, so happy,
and so full of light she promised to live and die
for you.
This time she kept her baby
and let the daddy go.

Hearing this part makes me breathe a little easier.
Maybe all this trouble

wasn't my fault, my doing.
I feel brave enough to say,
I wish he'd come back to us, my daddy.
He's not so bad.
Do you think he would?
If Mama could be nicer,
more fun?

Gram shakes her head.
Your mama did her best,
I guess,
to make a steady life for you.
It isn't always easy,
it isn't always fun
to be a mama.

All this talk about Mama
makes me lonely,
makes me wish I was there
—can't imagine her here—
wish I was back together with my mama
in the city.

Sometimes I miss that life
in the hard mean city.
I miss walking in a crowd bumping together

with so many shoulders, so many elbows,
being carried along
by the rhythm of so many feet,
by the music of so many voices,
by the mirror of so many eyes.

Taking my place on a bench or a curb
with a whole line of bodies
makes me feel like one of them,
feel like somebody,
like I belong.

I miss the soundtrack of the city
spilling out from ragtag music makers on the sidewalk,
hoping for a dollar but settling
for a smile.

I miss the smells of spicy sausages and sauerkraut,
beans with rice and fried bananas,
sweet hot doughnuts rolled in cinnamon,
snow cones every color
served from big-wheeled carts
rolling by.

I miss the rushing rumble underfoot
of subway trains

roaring through dark tunnels,
a thousand black umbrellas
sprouting up like mushrooms
when skyscraping buildings snag passing rainclouds
and open up the sky.

Don't forget, Phoebe Rose,
I tell myself when I start to think this way
—I have to tell myself
because there's no one else to tell me—
don't forget,
the city isn't easy, isn't gentle,
it isn't often nice.

I remember all right.
Feeling zero-down-underwater-in-the-bottom-of-a-hole
too scared to close your eyes—
that feeling tends to stick.
But there's something else in the city
that makes you hum, makes you tick,
keeps you ready, up on tiptoe,
expecting something big,
keeps you wide awake,
like a coffee pot plugged in.
But you have to have
the beans for it.

Giving What You Have

Every Friday afternoon
I walk with Gram
to her little bitty church
to help sort giveaway clothes and food
to bag for the poor.
Turns out hard-luck folks
live here in the country too.

A woman comes in with three little
ragtag boys,
and her with a belly out to here,
number four.
Gram smiles and calls them
all by name.
Mona, Michael, Bradley, Joe,
meet my granddaughter here,
Phoebe Rose.

At first I feel like a Friday afternoon
church phony,
like it shows somehow in my face
that I'm a taker,
not a giver.
While Mona picks out three good shirts,
powdered milk, and spaghetti,

I teach those boys
some knock-knock jokes
and how to draw a train
that disappears down the track.
It's not much,
but it makes me feel good
giving what I have.
It's all that I can give.

Compensation

On our way back to Gram's
giggle noises rise from the graveyard.
No ghosts out there,
just a sucky-faced girl about my age
and an older boy smoking,
both huddled down hiding
behind the headstones.

I giggle too,
but Gram goes scowly.
Don't be thinking that way, Phoebe Rose,
at your tender age.
Don't you start up so young
like your mama.

I march on ahead fast
and don't say a word.
Why scold me? I'm not my mama.
It wasn't me smooching and smoking,
disrespecting those bones.

Back at Gram's
I still feel out of sorts.
Why can't Mama come home?
Here?
To us?
Now?

Gram pulls a shivery big breath and says,
I made it too hard for your mama, Phoebe Rose.
I didn't tell it to you full and all before.

Gram pours us each a drink
of deep, cold chokecherry juice
and I settle in to listen
to Gram's new, improved version of the past.

The first time your mama left, she didn't just leave
on her own, I told her to go,
to get out and go far away
to live her trashy life

where I wouldn't have to see it.
And don't come crying
when it all goes sour, I told her.
I wish I hadn't said it, but I did.
So she left and didn't come back,
couldn't come back after that.

Oh!
That is a different story.
Walking out or ordered out
makes two different tales.

Now you're my compensation, Phoebe Rose,
Gram says.
Life always gives back a compensation
for what it takes away.

I'm not sure I like being compensation.
It feels like second prize.
Like something you have to settle for
instead of what you really want.

Don't you still want my mama back?

Of course I do, Gram says.
I always kept hoping she'd come back

someday.
Then her daddy passed
and I felt so bad he was gone
before his baby girl got her life turned around.
I wanted to put the blame on somebody,
so that somebody was your mama.
I was mad, so mad!
She even stole cash money from me!
Though I knew it was that bum
put her up to it.
I was mad, so mad!
She chose to spoil her life when I dreamed
so much good for her
that was never going to happen.
I built up a wall of words too high
for your mama to climb up and over,
too high to even try.

I don't ask any more questions.
I know how hard it is to tell a whole bad story
all at once. I've heard enough
for now.
I just hold Gram's hand.
I can see how truly sad she is.
She only wanted good,
but it's all gone bad

and there's so much too much to undo,
to forgive, to forget, to fix.

But I can't help thinking,
witch talk or true,
if Gram was so hard, so stone-cold stubborn
with her own baby girl,
when push comes to shove,
how's she going to treat me?

I don't see a happy-ever-after ending coming here,
not for Gram or Mama or me.
No end in sight of mamas giving up their babies.
No end in sight of trouble.

Life at Ruby's Place

I like the days I spend at Ruby's place.
So much commotion, so much fun!
Walter fixes engines, so he's got
tractors, trucks, and cars
half apart, doors open everywhere.
We climb in and out,
take the wheel, honk the horn.
Sometimes he gets after us, but mostly
it's okay.

Deena laughs and says her job
is chasing babies.
That Walter and Deena are the sort who can never
get enough of babies,
foster, born to them, adopted.
It's just the way they are.
From what I've seen
those are some lucky babies getting chased
and caught up here.
Nobody's said how many babies there are
all told. Some are grown and gone.
Ruby's in the middle of seven
at home just now.

The oldest do for the youngest,
but being in the middle's good, Ruby says,
makes it easy to slip away.

Mostly we slip away to the orchard
where we can pull ourselves into the crooked arms
of those apple trees and draw.

Sometimes we slip to the goat pen.
You have to watch those butting heads
and guard the gate real careful
or those rowdy critters head straight

for Deena's flowerbeds and climb
right on top of Walter's cars.

Sometimes we slip on over to the rabbits
when a new litter's being born.
Such tiny little things lined up to their mama,
all pink and hairless
like a string of bubblegum cigars.
I hate to think how most of them end up
on the dinner table, fried, baked, stewed.
I'd like to open those cages,
let the rabbits run!
I'm glad at least
they don't have to test hairspray.
Three squirts in each eye,
you're done!

If there's no rabbit on it,
I like Ruby's dinner table fine.
I like a crowd of people eating all together.
Walter teases, Deena laughs at everything.
Sometimes food flies!

When I get back to Gram's
I feel a little low
with all the quiet.

I'm reminded this might not be
my home
for very long.
My birthday's coming soon.
My number twelve is nearly here.
Is Mama?

The list I make of what I'll take in case I have to run
is short, I don't need much.
The list I make of what I'll leave behind and miss
is shorter, one word:
everything.
I try to think what I'll say to any nosy one I meet
along the way.
Where I come from, where I'm going?
I wonder, really, where that is?

So the days pass,
and day by day I feel myself growing
like the corn in Gram's garden,
taller, stronger, fuller,
close to ripe.

Turning Twelve

This day, my day, the day of my being born
twelve years ago, dawns
bright and steamy hot.
I feel heavy, edgy, slow, but in a hurry,
like something's round the corner
and maybe not.

I thought maybe she'd slip
in late last night
and surprise me this morning
first thing.
Looks like I'll have to be surprised
a little later.

All day long I fight a bad case of the jimmies
while the hours of my birthday
slide fast away.
Gram stirs up a big bowl of potato salad
and slices up a ham.
Walter and Deena show up
with a plate of chocolate cupcakes and fruit
in a wiggly jiggly red ring mold.
Ruby brings paper party hats all around
with a special one for me.
I want to tell Gram to set a place

for Mama,
but I know I couldn't swallow
all this birthday fun
with an empty plate, empty chair,
my own eyes looking empty
at the place where she should be.
So much nothing
weighs my heart down heavy.

I try to keep on smiling
when I open up my presents.
Brand-new underwear from Gram,
fine, fresh paper from Ruby,
and socks from her folks.
I try to keep on smiling
when Deena points her camera in our faces—
everybody yells, Cheese!
I try to keep on smiling
when Gram lights a candle on my cupcake,
when they all sing happy birthday,
when they say, Make a wish.
I stare and stare at that flame
till it burns a hole in my heart
and wishes melt away
like wax.

The Party Is Over

The party is over
when I say, Sorry,
but I have to take this ache in my stomach
off to bed.
It's true,
I do have an ache
like a big hot spoon stirring up some trouble,
stirring up the worry deep inside.
But I'm not heading for my bed,
it's the door I'm aiming for
and the road
that will take me
to my mama.

Before the guests take their leave
I'm packing underwear and socks,
my brand-new paper and some pencils,
a handful of egg money
from Gram's blue coffee can
—just like that thief my mama—
plus a few crimson feathers from the Ladies
so my eyes will always remember
that color.
I stuff all these necessary things
in a runaway bag.

But Ruby takes me by surprise
when she walks right in and sees
me packing up to run.

Will you tell? I ask.

Don't go, is Ruby's answer.
If you leave you'll have to take me along.
And I don't want to go, Ruby says,
don't want to hurt my folks and Gram.
You say we're close as sisters, Phoebe Rose,
both with our ruby-rose-red names,
and sticking close together is something
sisters do for each other
when they can.

I like that Ruby wants to help.
I like the thought of keeping her close,
but it would make more trouble,
taking her along,
and I don't need that.
So I say something mean
to make her let me go
off alone.

You're not my sister, Miss Ruby,
you don't know about

my mama or my daddy or my real true life
in the city where I come from and belong
and it's none of your business,
so good-bye.
I turn my back fast to hide my face,
waiting to hear the door slam.

Instead
I hear Ruby's voice gone quiet,
saying, Phoebe, did you know you got some trouble
on your backside?
Just thought you should know.

Then she leaves me alone
with my trouble.

Big Trouble

It's trouble all right.
A bloody big red trouble spot
growing on my backside,
changing all my plans.
I can't leave now
with blood, my blood, leaking out, soaking through
for all the world to see
I'm not just a little child anymore.

It caught me by surprise
—some fine birthday surprise,
this grownup messy woman business now,
when I need to find that mama.
I should have left sooner.
No!
That mama should be here with me
now,
when I need her.
Instead it's up to me. I have to clean myself up,
have to wash the red from my clothes,
have to find what I need to catch the flow.
And that big hot spoon in my gut
that I thought was worry
keeps stirring up the bloody, cramping
trouble and the tears.

What's the matter with me anyway?
What's going on in my head, in my heart,
that makes me want to run
from the things I've always wanted most
now I've got them?
Here at last I've got a safe, clean house
with my very own bed,
home-cooked food,
plenty of socks and undies all lined up

in a drawer with my pencils,

a true, art-loving sister-friend close by,

and I want to shuck it all

and run.

Run to Mama.

I always figured

I'd be sharing my dream-come-true

of a real, true home

with Mama.

How can any home be home-sweet-home

without Mama?

Instead of taking to the road

I take to my bed and wait

for the racing, chasing thoughts in my head

to tire themselves out and let me sleep.

Facing Up to Gram

Gram lets me be

till I'm ready to face her again.

I take my place

next to her on the porch

and we do some wordless rocking for a time.

At last I have to ask.
Didn't you expect she'd show up today,
same as me?

Gram sighs deep before she answers.
I don't have expectations for your mama
anymore, Phoebe Rose.
Just wait and see what happens,
let it flow.

But she's my mama!
I stomp my feet hard
on the floorboards and set my rocker
flying, nearly flipping.
She should have been here
on my birthday, no excuse!

I know you're hurting, Gram says,
but there's no fixing other folks,
no use expecting more than they can give.

Before I can stop myself
I ask what I don't want to know.
What if she never comes back?
What if my mama
is gone for good? Then what
will happen to me?

I guess you'll be stuck with me, Phoebe Rose.
My place can be yours
for as long as you need it.
I guess that's better
than nothing.

Inside I'm as mad at myself
as I am at Mama.
Mad at me for nearly running off
from Gram like a thankless thief.
Mad at me for acting like some sorry
whipped dog always coming back
for more.
Trying to run to the mama
who runs from me.
No more, I decide.
That's done.
Let her come to me
if she wants.
See how she likes being sent away
by her baby, no baby anymore.
I'll just stay here if I please,
and I do. I'll live with Gram
and go to school with Ruby.

I stand and stretch, feeling loose,
feeling free at last
of that mama.

Waking the Moon

Night by night the moon wakes up.
From the window I watch
as the moon crawls up through the trees,
red-orange at first, then yellow, then white.
Rising, swelling, like a breast full to bursting,
the milky full moon blooms high
in the star-studded night.

Too full to hold all the bright white light,
the moon spills down a silver path across the water.
It flows across the lake and into Gram's house,
right through the window and onto the floor,
stars and moon in a pearly broth.

Together with Gram I float out the door
on the river of light and down to the lake.
On the moonlit shore we shed our clothes and slip right in,
splashing, singing, diving, floating,
not under the moon but in it.
At first I think I'm dreaming when I look up

and see not the Man in the Moon
but the mama.
There she is:
Mama.
My real-live-in-the-flesh
Mama.

Baby's Back

Gram's hands fly up to her mouth.
You're home! she cries.
At last my baby's home!

Baby? I never thought of my mama
as anybody's baby. But I suppose mamas
never stop thinking that way.

Gram rises up from the water,
pulls her dress on fast,
and rushes to her baby.
I stay down low in the water,
just my nose poking up like a turtle.

I'd about given up on my baby,
Gram says.

But that baby, my mama,

folds up her arms and takes a step back.

You gave up a long time ago, Mama says,

with a snarly edge to her voice.

I said I'd come when I could

and I did.

Old Full Moon Lake isn't exactly on the main line.

Had to take a late bus

and hitch out here.

I know, I know, Gram says,

ignoring Mama's sassy mouth.

I just didn't know how much longer

Phoebe Rose could wait,

how much longer she'd put up

with her old country Gram.

Then I guess I got here just in time

this time, Mama says,

before you give her away too.

Wait a minute here!

I know my mama has a way

of looking for a fight, making a fight

when she can't find one.

But this brings me out of the lake shoulder high

shaking water from my ears.
Who gave who away?
When? Why?
I'm old enough to hear it all!
But now those two are too busy squawking
at each other
to pay me any mind.

Gram wobbles, but she stands
and talks right back to my mama.
You everlasting, exasperating girl!
Gram explodes,
both hands waving in the air
like a pair of startled birds all aflutter.
Then they fall.

Mama's arms stay crossed
and her head is bobbing,
just egging Gram on.

But Gram pulls a deep breath,
lets her words out slow,
in a pleading sort of way.
You agreed it was best
that way. Agreed you weren't ready,
signed the papers saying so. Besides,

it was all too hard on your daddy,
too hard on his heart.

Stop, Mama says.
I don't need to hear about that heart
I stopped.
That heart I broke so bad
it finally stopped beating
altogether.

You killed your daddy? I ask.

According to your Gram.

I didn't mean it, Gram says,
never meant it that way.

Now Gram's looking woozy.
She's swaying,
looking nearly ready to fall.

Taking Baby Back

Never mind that now,
Mama says.
Come on out, Phoebe Rose.
Hurry up.

So I splash on out
and stand there dripping and shaking,
not from cold
but from wanting those arms, Mama's arms,
to wrap me round and carry me up.
Didn't she want her mama that way too?
No matter all the crazy talk.
But we freeze like three stuck statues.

Mama comes to life
when she turns wide-eyed to look at me.
You've grown, Phoebe Rose, she says,
looking my new baby-woman self
all up and down.

Grown!
That's all she has to say?
I want to shake that mama good!
I want to slap that mama all the way to Full Moon Lake.
But she's already here—really here!—
that mama, my mama,
just like she said.
I'll come for you soon, she said,
on some soon tomorrow.
I'll come for you soon when I can.
I want to hug her,

that mama, my mama, and hold on tight,
tie her up tight,
like I would that dog I'll never have,
like I forgot to do with Daddy.

I want Mama to promise
never again to send me off,
never ever leave me behind
again.

Push and Pull

Instead,
Mama reaches out for me—
too late. I pull away.
You missed my birthday!
I turned twelve last week,
in case you forgot.

Then I run,
straight to Gram's house and into my bed.
I know it's as far as I'll get
for now.

Mama's right behind me.
Wait! I have something

for you, Phoebe Rose, Mama says
to the lump that's me
hiding flat-out quiet underneath a quilt.

I don't want to see it, I say,
but I do.
I try to muster up mad feelings,
but now they just lie low.

Okay, Mama says, maybe later.
I'll leave this box right here on the table,
right here on the table with your drawings.

While Floddie purrs and paws at me
underneath the quilt I lie still and quiet,
listening to Mama shuffling papers.
Drawings, she called them,
not doodles.
That gets me thinking.

Those drawings on the table
are mine all right.
Drawings I never meant for Mama to see.
They're drawings of the two of us
all fierce and mean and swimming
in a deep dark sea of blood and tears,
trying to save ourselves from drowning.

In those nasty old pictures
I left on the table
we're scrambling for our lives,
my mama and me,
fighting for a place on the lifeboat.
But the boat's not a real kind of boat,
it's that big old broken-down everlasting
burden of our lives,
the one that was up to me to keep,
hold fast, hold tight, and I didn't—
the suitcase.
It's the only thing in sight that floats,
so we're struggling in the waves
to claim a place on that suitcase for ourselves,
my mama and me,
but there's only room for one.
In the very last picture
I left on the table
in the boat
there's
only
me.

A Fancy Little Something

Maybe Mama got slapped in the face

by those pictures

from my angry heart,

but I got the wind knocked clean out of my gut

when I saw the little something,

the fancy little something,

Mama left for me.

The box.

A big white bakery box.

Inside, a fancy white cake, three layers at least,

pink roses on the top.

A stiff white paper keeping-cake

with tissue-paper flowers, tiny beads and buttons,

and ribbon ringed around,

looped like strings of sugar frosting.

Twelve pink pipe-cleaner candles poked up on top.

It's not the same old fold-up cake from the suitcase.

Mama didn't just pull this

from a trash can at the bus station

and add a few more candles.

This cake's fresh and new.

Mama worked long and hard

to make this new fancy keeping-cake for me.

All the while she was holding me
in her mind, Phoebe Rose,
holding me in her heart,
making plans
one way or another.
Suddenly I'm wondering if this is
a sorry-I-sent-you-off-and-missed-your-birthday sort of cake
or a cake that means I-just-came-to-say-good-bye.

Maybe I should have said
hello a little nicer.
Maybe now I've chased that mama off
for good.

I peek out the door
and there they are,
my mama and her mama in the rockers.
But things don't look right.
Gram is slumping, half slid out of her chair,
and Mama's eyes are popping
at what she sees.
By the time I get myself out on the porch
that Gram is making a funny gurgling
noise in her throat and twitching
too much, like a fish.

My mama just holds her own head
in her hands and wails.

I see Mama's no good
when things go bad, this bad,
so I take off running
to Ruby's.

Waiting

While Walter drives to the doctor
with my mama and Gram,
Deena and Ruby keep watch with me
in the shadowy light
of Gram's kitchen.
I like the heavy warmth of Floddie
in my lap,
but the sitting still and waiting
while the clock crawls around
is fidget-making, thumb-twiddling work.

We might as well bake, Deena says,
eyeing a bowl of ripe cherries.
How about a pie?
You girls can try your hand
at a crisscross crust
for the top.

I don't like the thought of food,
but my hands are happy
being busy.
I push the waiting off
by its old dark self
to the backroom corners of my mind.

First we work at pitting
those firm, plump cherries
till our fingers turn black-red.

Ruby shows me how to sift together flour and salt
in a bowl for a pastry crust.
Next we cut in the lard with a pair of knives
till crumbles form,
then a little cold-water sprinkle
pulls the dough together in a ball.

On a floured towel spread on the table
Deena rolls the rolling pin this way
and that way fast across the dough.
Ready for a pie plate, Phoebe Rose, she says.
Can you fetch one from that shelf?

I stand on tiptoes reaching up
to the top of Gram's sideboard,

shamed to think I've been here before,

reaching for the old blue coffee can

hiding behind the pie plates.

This time my slippery fingers are slippery with lard.

The pie plate gets away,

landing hard—too hard—on the floor.

That plate will never hold a pastry crust again.

Deena says she'll find another,

not to fret.

But it seems so sad,

this one last straw of a pie plate

gone to pieces.

I sit down among the ruins

and sob.

It's like my life

keeps falling off the shelf

and breaking into pieces

and there isn't enough

glue in the world

to put it back together.

Mosaics

It's okay, Ruby says,

kneeling down beside me.

You know about mosaics?

Then Ruby shows me how to take up
all the little broken pieces of a plate
and glue them down together
in a new sort of way
with spaces in between.

What you get is not an old mended plate
trying to look the same as it was
but a whole new thing
you never saw before.
A fine, new, pretty thing.

When things come apart
it's your chance to
rearrange the pieces, Ruby says.

Pretty soon I hear myself talking,
letting fly all the words,
all the feelings, all the hurts and the scares,
spitting out
all the anger and the secrets
of my life,
like the pits tucked deep
in the flesh of those sweet, dark cherries.

When I run out of steam
I'm too dry to cry.

I expect now Ruby and her folks will give up
on such a sorry lot of people
who keep handing off their babies,
keep running off, dying off,
breaking each other's hearts
like so many pie plates.
I expect Floddie will be next to leave me,
then the chickens.

Instead of giving up
Deena and Ruby hold me tight.
We know all that, Phoebe Rose, they say.
We know all that and more.

More?
Just when I think I've hit
the bottom of the bottom,
somebody pulls the rug
again.

The Last of It

Turns out that sister of mine,
the baby Mama gave away,
didn't get given to just any-old-body.
Mama didn't drop it in the trash

or leave it in the lost and found,

she put it in Gram's good care.

Mama said she'd come back soon,

but she didn't.

When my grandaddy passed,

Gram lost her heart for babies for a while.

She let that baby go,

adopted out to strangers.

The way things worked then,

it had to be a secret.

When mamas gave up their babies

they never knew where they went.

When Mama finally came looking for her baby

the law said no,

she had no more right to be the mama.

That's not fair!

My mama couldn't have her own baby?

I can't say what's fair, Deena says.

That baby has a family and a home

with good-hearted folks.

Fair or not, sometimes it's best

to let things be.

The phone cries out just then

with news from Walter at the hospital

that Gram is still with us.
Her heart didn't give up after all.
It was a spell of sky-high blood pressure
that knocked her to the floor.
She'll bounce back in time.

While Deena and Walter have more words about Gram,
Ruby, who's gone mighty quiet,
pulls me close and talks real soft
so only I can hear.
Maybe someday, Phoebe Rose,
that sister of yours will come looking for you,
when the time is right,
when she's ready.

I look deep in Ruby's eyes
to see if she's telling me more
than she's saying.
But I can't quite see
to the bottom of it all.

Sorting It Out

All this big news,
good and bad mixed together,
gives me that slapped-up feeling in my head.

It needs time to settle down
and come together
in a way I can get hold of
and roll into shape.

After the beans are spilled
Ruby and Deena
both look at me, nervous,
hang on me, pace after me.
They wring their hands,
they laugh and cry
and ask again and again
if I'm okay.

I tell them, All I know is
I need time to make some sense of this
alone
before I face my mama.
So please let me be.

I take up my running bag,
in case it comes to that,
and head for the door
to get some space.

That's when I stumble on the sound
of Deena's voice.

I know you've got a whole lot to swallow,
Phoebe Rose.
But you don't have to choke on it
if your heart is open,
if pride doesn't close the door.

I'm pounding down the back steps by now,
but that Deena doesn't give up.
She leans out the door
and calls after me, Phoebe Rose,
you may have to wash it down with tears,
but you can swallow the moon
if you have to.

Thinking Straight with Chickens

I get as far as the chicken coop
and decide that's as good a place
as any to think.
So I mull it over in my mind
with Floddie in my lap.
I brood on it in my heart
with the Crimson Ladies at my feet.
They listen up without a fuss
while I argue with myself out loud
and ponder with myself all quiet-like

on paper with my pencils,

trying to see it all clear

so I can see the next thing.

As far as anybody knows,

Mama's baby, my big sister,

might have gone anywhere.

Far away or near.

Maybe just to the other side

of Full Moon Lake,

to good-hearted, baby-loving people

like Walter and Deena.

Maybe, probably,

I hope and pray

they took my mama's baby, my big sister,

and raised her as their own

to this day.

Ruby!

My sister Ruby!

Yes! I can imagine this, want this, need this

to be true. Not just for myself.

For Mama.

Rearranging the Pieces

I notice that it's raining outside

when a spit of water splashes down through the roof

onto my paper.

It seems to me that a roof overhead

is a good thing to have,

whether you're a chicken or not.

I know that good, solid roofs, even old, cracked, leaky ones,

come and go in this life.

But I can't run away from the house of my own heart.

I have to know how to feel at home

inside myself

if I'm going to feel at home

anywhere.

It's time to quit hiding under quilts

of imagined hurts

and scraps of injured pride.

And I have to leave the door open a bit

for good-hearted folks

trying to do their best.

I think it's better to sit rocking on the porch

ready with a welcome for the people in your life

while you have them.

From the straw beneath the Ladies' perch

I pick up bits of broken egg shells

all speckled different shades of brown.

These shells that lost their egg shape

I can't put back together

like they were.

But I can rearrange the pieces

in endless fine designs with spaces in between,

in ways an egg never thought before to be.

Mosaics, Ruby said.

Not second-best,

something different altogether,

a surprise!

First you draw it broken,

then you draw it mended.

Not just like it was, something different

you never saw.

Like the scraps of Gram's old dresses

patched together in a brand-new quilt.

If you can draw it new, you can dream it new.

If you can dream it, you can make it.

Imagine!

Redo myself.

Renew myself.

Me, Fancy Phoebe Rose,

remade!

Where does that leave me
with Mama?
I can't fix her
or change her,
but maybe
I can give her a little something
to make a little peace
with Mama, her mama, and me.

Meeting up with Ruby

In the orchard, Ruby brings me
the photo I want.

Here's the birthday-party picture of the two of us
you asked for, Phoebe Rose. Can't say
it's your very best smile.

I stare at the pair of us
grinning in our party hats. Ruby's right
about my smile.
It's okay, I say to Ruby, I can fix it.
I pull out the scissors that I brought
for this occasion,
causing great alarm in Ruby's eyes.

Stop! You'll spoil it! Ruby cries,
and she snatches back the photo.

Ruby!
I don't intend to cut that picture!

Then what's the scissors for?

Your hair.
Quickly then I take a snippet
from her head.

Phoebe Rose! You gone crazy?

Now it's your turn, I tell Ruby,
and I put the scissors in her hand.

Ruby still looks puzzled.
What's this all about?

Ruby, I don't know yet if I'm staying
here or leaving.
But if I don't see you for a while,
I want each of us to have
something of the other to hold on to,
to remind us that we're sisters deep inside.

At that, Ruby gets a little weepy.
Her hands are shaking
as she helps herself to my hair.
Did you know, Phoebe Rose,
that I'm one of the adopted ones?
Not natural-born to the folks I have now.

I figured so, I tell Ruby.

I understand that people can't
always live
with the parents that had them, Ruby says.
Life shuffles folks around
like a deck of cards,
and I've been dealt a lucky hand
here, where I am.
But there's always that big question mark.
So much I'll probably never know.

I hug her close,
my sister Ruby.
We're somehow tied tight together
by our unanswered questions.
We vow that our traded locks of hair
will keep us tied forever.

Back at Gram's
I fix my smile the way I meant to,
on paper.
From that photo,
I draw my own picture
of two fine-smiling sisters,
together again and forever.
A picture for that mama,
my mama, to have.

Gram's Coming Back

Gram's coming back from her spell
pretty good, the doctor says.
If she eases up on herself
and takes her pills,
she'll soon be back in those cowboy boots
clucking at her hens again.

Does she live all alone? the doctor asks.
She'll need some help for a while.
Someone to make her mind
doctor's orders.
Can someone stay for a while?
Think it over, doctor says
when no one answers.

Must be someone
who has a helping heart.

Now I see my poor little Gram's no witch,
no more than the rest of us.
She's just trying to do
what's right
and sometimes gets it wrong.

Settling Up with Mama

When finally Mama and me
come face to face
we act shy and polite as strangers
in our rockers on the porch,
talking about the weather and the birds
and nothing much important.
I have to find out what Mama was planning for me
before Gram went down.
Was she coming to collect me
or dropping in to say good-bye?
And what's she thinking now?
I don't want to go with my mama
if she feels she's no-choice stuck
with me.
I want to be wanted

by my mama.
But she doesn't say a word.

Guess it's up to me,
so I pull a deep breath and jump right in.
Thank you, Mama, I say, for my cake,
my birthday keeping-cake.

Sorry it was late, Phoebe Rose.
Sorry I was late.
I've been so wrapped up in my troubles
I couldn't see my way through.
I pounded those streets in the city
so hard, Phoebe Rose,
all through the hot summer
till finally I found a new kind of shelter,
transition they call it,
like a bridge from a place where the answer
is always no
to a place where the answer is
maybe yes, maybe so.
If I sign up
they'll take a chance on me
with some schooling and some work
for real pay, even trips to the dentist.

What About Me?

I nod to my mama and try to smile,
but my mind is racing ahead
to my own next thing.
Will Gram be well enough to keep me?
Could Ruby's family take me in?
Will I have to start down that homeless
trail of foster homes?
If only my eyes were longer!
By now I see I'm rocking so hard and fast
I'm nearly sailing off the porch.
Settle down, Phoebe Rose,
I tell myself.
You don't need to see
the whole big picture at once.
Put the pieces in place,
let them find their place
one piece at a time.

Looking out from Gram's porch
at all the green, I'm reminded of moss,
Ruby's moss,
and reminding myself to be like that,
a whole fancy little world to myself,
at home anywhere.

Letting Mama Go

Mama's voice pulls me back.

You know life in the city's been hard for me,

Phoebe Rose,

but the coming back here was harder.

A grown person can't keep hiding

or bringing home her troubles to her mama.

I swore I never would!

But here I am again, and look what's happened,

what I did now to your Gram.

How's she going to manage herself now?

Everything I do makes things worse, Phoebe Rose.

Mama shakes her head

can't look me in the eye.

My life's a mess, Phoebe Rose,

a mess I can't seem to undo, and now

you're nearly grown

and I'm messing your life too.

I'm so tired out and it's all so hard.

Maybe we should just forget it.

Probably you'd be better off

with anybody else than me.

So, it seems Mama's come to ditch me.

She's trying to let me down easy,

trying mostly to be easy on herself,

setting up a fence that leaves me out.

Probably she planned to breeze in,

say a quick good-bye,

have a nice life, Phoebe Rose,

and be on her way.

But I can see the days Mama's spent

with Gram at the hospital

have sucked the wind from her sails.

She feels the blame for Gram's spell;

still, she doesn't want to face the shame straight on.

She wants to make it her excuse now

to leave me here as Gram's keeper.

I take a deep breath and tell myself,

Mama's going to do

what Mama's going to do, Phoebe Rose.

Why make things harder?

So I take Mama's hand real gentle.

I know all about it, I tell her,

I know all about it all.

Knowing's better.

And it's all

all right.

A Little Something for Mama

We both lean back in our rockers,
shaky from that kind of talk.
Now there's only one thing left
to do.

I have something for you, Mama.
A little something that I made.

When I hand over my new creation
I get a sudden stomach-dropping,
stepping-off-a-cliff type of feeling
that this whole idea
is wrong, all wrong.
Part of me wants to fly to the chicken coop,
hide my head under the nearest quilt.
· I start hardening up my heart,
expecting cold, hard words to fly
back at me from Mama,
the same way it happened
when I made those paper-doll clothes
that landed in the trash
such a long time ago.

But the bigger part of me says,
You stay put, Phoebe Rose,

stop acting like a child.
If you truly believe
that the art of making art
is necessary for you
to go on living your life
in any happy way,
if you truly believe that your art
makes you see beyond
make-believe
to the real true heart
of believing,
you stay put
and see this through.

So I sit and watch my mama
study the little box I made.
She handles it as gently
as an old china cup.

Looks like a little bitty suitcase,
Mama says as she traces her fingers over tiny hinges,
around the latches and the handle,
all made from an old brown box
that still smells of baking sugar
covered over with grocery-bag paper
and trimmed with cut-out bits of shoelaces, cornhusks,

stray ends of this and that
found around Gram's place.

Who showed you how to do
something like this? Mama asks.

You did, Mama.
I looked long and hard at the clever fold-out,
pop-up cake parts you made,
and I made a suitcase shape instead.

The look on Mama's face
when she turns her sad, lost eyes on me
pulls the plug on the words
stored deep inside of me,
and out they gush.

Mama, I've had all summer here
to think about the suitcase,
how I lost it and your baby's hair inside.

What's gone is gone, Phoebe Rose.
You didn't—

No, Mama!
I've been dragging it along

all this time in my mind,

that everlasting suitcase,

studying it with my new artist's eyes.

Mama, when that suitcase first went missing,

you gave up,

said we were down to nothing.

Nothing left but pride.

Phoebe, I don't need—

Listen, Mama!

All summer long here on Full Moon Lake

I've been looking at that suitcase

with my deeper-looking eyes

and I found that pride

isn't the end of it after all.

Open the suitcase, Mama,

and you'll find one thing more.

Mama Looks Deeper

Mama twists her mouth

like she's running low on patience,

but she slips the latch on that made-over

brown baking sugar box

and finds an envelope inside

marked "Hope—yours for the taking."
Mama opens the seal and pulls out the picture
of Ruby and me.
Not the photo with the party hats
but a tidied-up drawing I made
with a true-to-life smile on my face.

That's me on my birthday
with Ruby, my good, best friend from across the lake,
Walter and Deena's middle girl, I tell Mama.
But she's more than a good, best friend,
she's a sister, my sister.
We feel that way, both of us.
It's like I found that lost baby of yours.
I want you to have this picture, Mama,
so you'll know
not only how it could have been
but how it is.
So, don't worry about me, Mama.
You got your hands full with your own self.

Mama squints like she's trying to pick her way
along a fog-thick path.
Phoebe Rose, are you sending me back
to the city alone?

Now I feel foggy.
I thought that's what you wanted, Mama.
That bridge is waiting
to take you somewhere.

It's for both of us, Phoebe Rose.
A room of our own,
with a key
and one more chance
for the two of us together.
Oh—something else
I almost forgot.
Every Thursday night the art lady comes
to the transition shelter place
with paint and clay and chalk.
Maybe we could try it
together, Phoebe Rose.
If you want.

It's hard to see things straight
when all you expect is crooked.
Finally I see
Mama's asking me, not telling.
I can't be sure it'll work
any better this time than before.
Mama's not very strong

on her own.

She might hook up with another

sweet-talking man

who turns things sour.

Or mess up all by herself.

But now I see that the things she tells me

or doesn't,

the promises she keeps or breaks,

aren't meant to hurt me.

Whatever happens next

with Mama and me,

I see another future after that,

a clear, sure future

for Ruby and me,

heading off to art school,

becoming what we want to be.

Still,

for right now

I like being chosen,

especially by my mama.

I try to squeeze out a yes,

but my voice is stuck

in a tight, floody puddle in my throat.

I see Mama's having the same sort of struggle,

but there's nothing more

that needs saying,

so we go

for a swim.

Feasting on Soul Moon Soup

Bobbing up and down with my mama

in Full Moon Lake I see

she's just another person

trying to keep her head above water.

What Mama needs now is

a little time-out at Gram's little place

on Full Moon Lake.

A little time-out, a little hand-holding,

heart-healing, softening up

of that cold, hard, stubborn pride

for both of them.

Then we'll give it one more try,

my mama and me,

on our own in the city,

a little stronger this time,

we'll try.

Maybe sometimes I want too much, need too much

from that mama, my mama,

when here she is just another soul
out swimming in the water.
I can't keep asking for more mama
than Mama can be.
And look at me—I'm nearly grown,
ready to be more of a mama to myself.
When that's not enough
then my art,
my soul-stretching, soul-saving, picture-making
art is a big enough mama for me.
Art will be my mama.
Art will be my home.

Now I stretch out flat on the smooth silver
surface of Full Moon Lake.
In that giant bowl of bright white light
I feast my soul
till I'm full enough to dream,
to imagine,
to hope,
for tomorrow and tomorrow,
endless days
filled with friends and songs and green tomato pie.

Now I know how to feed my own soul fat,
when it's been too lean too long.

With songs and pictures
to share with the people in my life
I can feed me, fill me,
belly and soul,
on soup of the full moon,
feed me full,
on soul
moon
soup.